D1537592

This edition first published in the U.S. in 1987
by Willowisp Press, Inc., 401 E. Wilson Bridge Road,
Worthington, Ohio 43085

Text © Mathew Price 1987
Illustrations © Errol Le Cain 1987

Designed and produced by Mathew Price Ltd,
242A Canbury Park Road,
Kingston upon Thames,
Surrey KT2 6LG

Printed in Hong Kong for Imago

Mathew Price

# THE CHRISTMAS STOCKINGS

*Illustrated by*
Errol Le Cain

**Willowisp Press**

It's Christmas Eve.
Santa Claus has come to fill
two little stockings with toys.
But there's no chimney.
How will he get down?
Can you help him?

Well, he's inside the house.
But there are no stockings here.
Where can he go now?

There are still no stockings. We'll have to help him again. Can you find another door?

A Christmas party! What fun.
But we can't stop here.
We have to find those stockings.
Where's the way out?

EXIT

Ouch! That was quite a drop!
Now, what's this? A toy shop?
Yes, it is. We'll never
find the stockings here.
Come on, Santa Claus,
it's getting late.

There they are!